This
Book Belongs
to...

_____

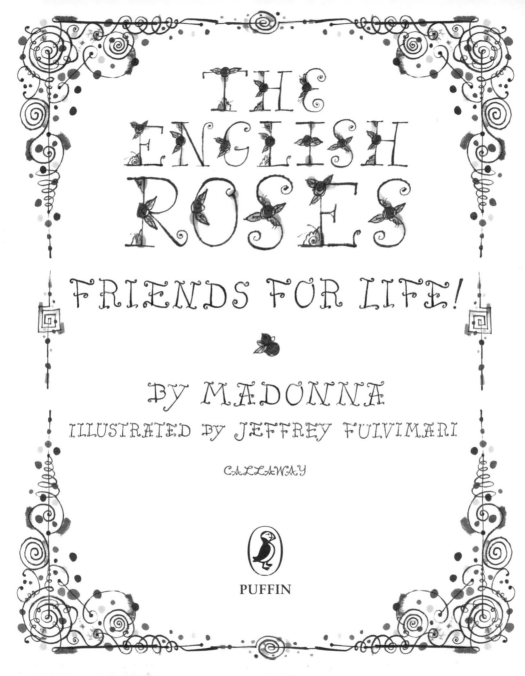

THE ENGLISH ROSES

FRIENDS FOR LIFE!

BY MADONNA

ILLUSTRATED BY JEFFREY FULVIMARI

CALLAWAY

PUFFIN

PUFFIN BOOKS

Published by the Penguin Group
Penguin Books Ltd, 80 Strand, London WC2R oRL, England
Penguin Group (USA) Inc., 375 Hudson Street, New York, New York 10014, USA
Penguin Group (Canada), 90 Eglinton Avenue East, Suite 700, Toronto, Ontario, Canada M4P 2Y3
(a division of Pearson Penguin Canada Inc.)
Penguin Ireland, 25 St Stephen's Green, Dublin 2, Ireland (a division of Penguin Books Ltd)
Penguin Group (Australia), 250 Camberwell Road, Camberwell, Victoria 3124, Australia
(a division of Pearson Australia Group Pty Ltd)
Penguin Books India Pvt Ltd, 11 Community Centre, Panchsheel Park, New Delhi – 110 017, India
Penguin Group (NZ), 67 Apollo Drive, Rosedale, North Shore 0632, New Zealand
(a division of Pearson New Zealand Ltd)
Penguin Books (South Africa) (Pty) Ltd, 24 Sturdee Avenue, Rosebank, Johannesburg 2196, South Africa

Penguin Books Ltd, Registered Offices: 80 Strand, London WC2R oRL, England

puffinbooks.com

First published in the USA in 2007
Designed by Toshiya Masuda and produced by Callaway Arts & Entertainment
First published in Great Britain in Puffin Books 2008
1 3 5 7 9 10 8 6 4 2

British Library Cataloguing in Publication Data
A CIP catalogue record for this book is available from the British Library

ISBN: 978–0–141–38378–1

All of Madonna's proceeds from this book will be donated to
Raising Malawi (www.raisingmalawi.org), an orphan-care initiative.

TABLE OF CONTENTS

We're the English Roses – Binah, Grace, Amy, Charlotte and Nicole. We're best friends who do everything together.

On the last day of school last year, our awesome year-seven teacher, Miss Fluffernutter, suggested we make a book listing all of our favourite things, people and memories. She told us that she and her friends made a similar book when they were our age, and she loves looking at it now. Well, we think anything Miss Fluffernutter does is the coolest, so all summer we passed this book around to one another and recorded everything – our biggest crushes, our favourite ice cream flavours, and especially our hopes and dreams for the future. We also included some special sections, like study tips, a British glossary for Grace, and a peek inside fashionista Amy's bag – even a postcard from foreign-exchange cutie Dominic de la Guardia!

We hope you have as much fun reading our book as we've had making it!

Cheers,

Binah Grace Amy
Charlotte Nicole

The Stars:
the English Roses

Binah
the serious one

Grace
the sporty one

Amy
the fashionista

Charlotte
the posh one

Nicole
the brainiac

Supporting Cast

Miss Fluffernutter
the coolest teacher ever

Fairy Godmother
the sassy one

Mr
Bina

Dominic
de la Guardia
the heartthrob

Bunny Love & Candy Darling
the dancing duo

Terry Ferguson
the naughty brother

Taffy &
Ferg
the

Mr Ferguson
the fiddle-playing
father

everyone

{ Vital Statistics }

Full name: Binah Rossi

Nickname: B

Birthday: 27 November

Astrological sign: Sagittarius

Birthplace: London

Eye colour: Blue

Hair colour: Blonde

Height: 145 cm

Family: Me and my papa — my mum died when I was very little.

Pet(s): None

Who is your BFF? The English Roses: Nicole, Amy, Charlotte and Grace.

Name one thing that you can do better than any of your friends.

Housework!

What is the best gift you ever received? Last year when Grace travelled around Europe with her family, she brought me back a bracelet with a charm from each country she had visited. It was so sweet of her to think of me throughout her trip.

When you grow up, what do you want to be?

A teacher.

You can't wait till the day you get to be a teacher, just like Miss Fluffernutter.

Worst habit: Giggling for no reason

What is one secret about you that only your closest friends know?

That I am colour-blind.

What is the most embarrassing thing that ever happened to you? Last week I was running late and quickly rubbed on some lip balm before leaving the house. People were giving me funny looks on the street and I couldn't figure out why. It was only when I got to school that my friends told me I'd used a tinted balm — and smeared my entire mouth, not just my lips, bright pink!

go Binah!

13

 **BINAH**

Heroes: *My mum*

Person/People you'd like to meet: *I wish I could travel back in time to meet Queen Elizabeth the First.*

Celebrity crush: *Bono*

Real-life crush: *Dominic de la Guardia*

IM name: *Bee*

What nail polish shade are you wearing today?
I don't wear nail polish.

Are your ears pierced? *no*

If you had to choose, which do you think best describes your personal style?

    a. Sporty   b. Funky   (c. Casual)   d. Classic   e. Dressy

Which best describes your personality?

    a. Girly girl   b. Tomboy   (c. Studious)   d. Fashionable   e. Goofy

Favourite lip gloss flavour: *I don't wear lip gloss.*

Fashion icon: Hmmm . . . I'm not that into fashion.
I love the way Charlotte dresses, though.

Favourite colour: pale blue

If your shoes did the talking, what would they say about you?

That I wear them a lot!

Favourite book: Anne of Green Gables

How do you want to celebrate your next birthday?

A tea party with the
English Roses.

What is your favourite thing in your room?

My doll

 # BINAH

Who is your favourite teacher? Miss Fluffernutter

What do you like to do after school? Hang out with the
English Roses before I go home to do chores.

What's your favourite after-school snack? crisps

Favourite food: toasted cheese
sandwiches

The yummiest ice cream flavour:

butterscotch

The yuckiest vegetable: turnips

Favourite pizza toppings:

I like cheese and tomato pizza.

You can't leave home without

a clip in my hair and a picture
of my mum in my bag.

my mum

18

What is your best physical feature?

I don't know ... you'll have to ask my friends that.

What is your guilty pleasure?

long, hot bubble baths

What is your favourite movie?

Oliver Twist.

What is your pet peeve? *spoiled brats*

What doesn't come easily to you?

fussing over my looks

If you found £10 on the street,

what would you do with the money?

Give it to my papa.

 # BINAH

How would you react if someone copied your work?

I'd be disappointed, but I wouldn't say anything.

What most often gets you in trouble?

Talking on the phone.

Favourite season: *Spring,*

when all the birds fly back

and all the flowers are in bloom.

Do you speak any languages besides English?

A bit of French, and I'm

planning to learn Spanish soon too.

Where do you want to live when you grow up?

London.

If you were stranded on a desert island, which three things would you want to have with you? Why? Actually, I'd want four — Nicole, Amy, Charlotte and Grace — because together we'd figure out a way to save ourselves.

What did you do over the summer? I went to visit my grandmother in Cornwall. We had the best time together!

Binah's Time-Saving Tips...

Since my mother died when I was very young, I've had to grow up a little bit faster than other girls my age. Running our household is my responsibility, and I've become something of an expert at doing things as efficiently as possible; that way, I can have even more time for fun things, like hanging out with the English Roses. Here are some tips that can help you manage your time more effectively too.

PACK A LUNCH THE NIGHT BEFORE

Keep frantic mornings in check by making your lunch the night before. Put everything in a lunch bag and keep it in the refrigerator overnight. In the morning, don't forget to slip it into your schoolbag before you leave!

LAY OUT YOUR CLOTHES THE NIGHT BEFORE

Figure out what you want to wear the next day and, if possible, lay it out on a chair the night before so it's all ready to go. If you want to be really organized, pick out your outfits for the entire week and write them down so you don't forget!

KEEP A PLANNER

It may sound silly, but a calendar or planner that you can carry around with you is a big time- (and life-) saver! Write down all of your homework assignments, extracurricular activities, and plans with friends so you don't forget anything.

CLEAN OUT YOUR SCHOOLBAG ONCE A WEEK

A weekly dusting out of your schoolbag can really work wonders. Throw or file away old tests or papers that can be confusing and get in the way of more recent assignments.

GET A BULLETIN BOARD

Post mementoes, keepsakes, photos, concert ticket stubs, and important flyers on a bulletin board in your room. It's a great way to cut down on paper clutter and to remind yourself of fun memories as well as exciting future events.

GRACE

{ Vital Statistics }

Full name: Grace Harrison

Nickname: Gracie

Birthday: 10 April

Astrological sign: Aries

Birthplace: Atlanta, Georgia, USA

Eye colour: Brown   Hair colour: Black

Height: 140 cm

Family: Mom, Dad and twin brothers, Matthew and Michael, 16 years old

Pet(s): I don't have any pets.

 **GRACE**

Who is your BFF? *Nicole, Amy, Charlotte and Binah*

Name one thing that you can do better than any of your friends.

That's easy – play sports!

What is the best gift you ever received?

My friends chipped in and got me a subscription to Sports Illustrated magazine. I love reading about all kinds of sports.

When you grow up, what do you want to be?

I want to be a soccer star, but it's called football here in England.

You can't wait till the day you *are allowed to go to football games without my parents. It will be so cool to go with my friends!*

26

Worst habit: I bite my nails.

What is one secret about you that only your closest friends know?

I sometimes pretend I'm grown-up and try on my mom's dresses.

What is the most embarrassing thing that ever happened to you?

It just happened the other day My backpack was open, and I accidentally dropped it, spilling everything. There was stuff everywhere, including my sports bra. Everyone saw it and laughed! It was super-horrible!

Heroes: David Beckham and Mia Hamm

GRACE

Person/People you'd like to meet: Venus and Serena Williams. They're awesome!

Celebrity crush: David Beckham

Real-life crush: The boys I know are lame. I don't like any of them.

IM name: GracieH

What nail polish shade are you wearing today?

I don't wear nail polish. Ever!

Are your ears pierced? No

If you had to choose, which do you think best describes your personal style?

a. Sporty   b. Funky   c. Casual   d. Classic   e. Dressy

Which best describes your personality?

    a. Girly girl   (b. Tomboy) c. Studious   d. Fashionable   e. Goofy

Favourite lip gloss flavour: Eww. I don't wear lip gloss!

Fashion icon: Maria Sharapova looks cool on and off the tennis court

Favourite colour: lavender

If your shoes did the talking, what would they say about you?

That girl can run!

How do you want to celebrate your next birthday? I would love to have a roller-skating party.

What is your favourite thing in your room?

My David Beckham poster. For sure!

GRACE

When you can't fall asleep, what do you think about?

I imagine playing the best game of my life and scoring the winning goal!

Favourite way to spend a rainy afternoon:

Having lunch with my best friends

Car you would like to drive someday:

Range Rover

Favourite book:

All of the Judy Moody books. They're so funny!

Three things you can't live without: 1. My poster of David Beckham, because he signed it

2. My favourite football

3. My best friends, Amy, Charlotte, Binah and Nicole

Which is your favourite subject at school, and which do you like least?

Science is my favourite subject, because you get to learn about things all around you. Music is my least favourite, because we're practising baby songs like 'Edelweiss'.

Whom do you sit next to at school?

This year, I sit next to Charlotte and a boy named Timothy. PE is the best part of the day!

 # GRACE

If you found £10 on the street, what would you do with the money?

I would add it to my savings. I'm saving up for a ticket to the World Cup in South Africa in 2010.

How would you react if someone copied your work?

 I would tease them mercilessly.

What most often gets you in trouble?

I leave my stuff all over the house and it makes my mom crazy!

Favourite season: Autumn, because it's football season.

Do you speak any languages besides English?

No

Where do you want to live when you grow up?

In a house that's close to a park, so I can play football whenever I want.

If you were stranded on a desert island, which three things would you want to have with you? Why?

1. My sneakers.
2. My football.
3. A mobile phone, so I could call my friends and my family to pick me up!

What did you do over the summer?

Since I was born in Atlanta, Georgia, we have lots of relatives there. Every summer we spend two weeks with my cousins. It's really fun.

35

Grace's Glossary

When I first moved to London from Atlanta, Georgia, I was always confused at the way English people spoke. Here's my handy glossary translating Brit-speak to Ameri-speak!

JOLLY OLD ENGLAND		U.S.A.
biscuits	=	cookies
brill	=	brilliant
brolly	=	umbrella
dustbin	=	trash can
flat	=	apartment
football	=	soccer
knackered	=	tired
knickers	=	underwear
lift	=	elevator
loo	=	restroom
Nosy Parker	=	busybody
ring	=	to call on the phone
rubbish	=	trash
telly	=	television
trainers	=	sneakers
tube	=	subway

My Saturday
by Grace

Here's my go at writing in Brit-speak:

When I woke up this morning I was so knackered I could hardly put on my knickers! Luckily, my fancy new trainers got me to the tube in half the time it would usually take. I hopped on and made it to my destination very quickly. While taking the lift to Nicole's grandmother's flat, I couldn't help jiggling my legs – the loo was calling my name! When I finally arrived, all of the English Roses were already there for our biscuit-making party. Unfortunately, since we were all glued to the telly, the biscuits burned in the oven! Sadly, we had to throw them in the dustbin with the other rubbish. I rang my mum to pick me up for football practice at 4 P.M. I scored a goal – brill! – but by the time practice was over, I was completely knackered once again!

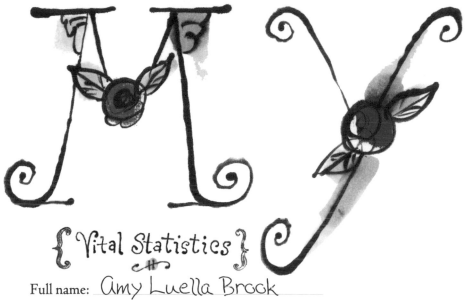

{ Vital Statistics }

Full name: Amy Luella Brook

Nickname: Carrots

Birthday: 4 August

Astrological sign: Leo

Birthplace: London

Eye colour: Green

Hair colour: Red

Height: 140 cm

Family: Dad; Mum and stepdad;
little sister, Chloe; and
a baby on the way

 AMY

Who is your BFF?

Nicole, Charlotte, Grace and Binah.

Name one thing that you can do better than any of your friends:

Accessorize.

What is the best gift you ever received?

For my tenth birthday, my mum
gave me her old Rolling
Stones concert T-shirt that
she wore as a teenager.

When you grow up, what do you want to be?

fashion designer

You can't wait till the day you:

attend my first fashion show.

Worst habit: I crack my knuckles a lot.

What is one secret about you that only your closest friends know? I am
terrified my father will get remarried and won't be
able to spend much time with me.

What is the most embarrassing thing that ever happened to you?

My mum brought me a to-die-for dress to wear to
a school dance, but I needed a bit of 'help' filling
out the top part. So, I used some wadded-up
tissues. But while I was dancing up a storm,
a few pieces of tissue fell out of the
dress. My face turned as red as my hair!

Heroes: Coco Chanel! I just read an article
about her; she founded the fashion
label Chanel and is responsible for all of
those fabulous little black dresses!

 **AMY**

Person/People you'd like to meet:

Stella McCartney

Celebrity crush: Orlando Bloom

Real-life crush: Ryan Hudson

IM name: KewlGrl82

What nail polish shade are you wearing today? Red Hot

Are your ears pierced? yep

If you had to choose, which do you think best describes your personal style?

a. Sporty   (b. Funky)   c. Casual   d. Classic   e. Dressy

Which best describes your personality?

a. Girly girl   b. Tomboy   c. Studious   d. Fashionable   (e. Goofy)

Favourite lip gloss flavour: Bubblegum

Fashion icon: Audrey Hepburn

Favourite colour: Red

If your shoes did the talking, what would they say about you?

That I have excellent taste.

How do you want to celebrate your next birthday?

Shopping spree with my best friends, and then all the bangers and mash we can eat!

What is your favourite thing in your room?

My old movie posters. I just love Audrey Hepburn!

When you can't fall asleep, what do you think about?

The autumn fashion collections.

Favourite way to spend a rainy afternoon: Shopping

Car you would like to drive someday:

Union Jack Mini Cooper

amy
Luella
Brook
Spring
Collection...

AMY

Favourite book:

<u>Vogue Fashion</u> – I love all of the pictures!

Three things you can't live without: make-up bag,

sketchbook, next month's fashion magazines

Which is your favourite subject at school, and which do you like least?

I love art class, especially when we get to

sketch and paint. I

HATE science – bugs

and frogs are gross.

Whom do you sit next to at school?

Nicole

PE is Ok if I can wear

my designer gym

clothes.

Sometimes a Rose's life can get VERY Heavy, dude...

44

What sports do you play? None - unless there are cute boys on the team.

Who is your favourite teacher?
Miss Fluffernutter

What do you like to do after school?
shop

What is your favourite after-school snack?
Cadbury Creme Eggs

Favourite food: Fish and chips

The yummiest ice cream flavour:
Mint Chocolate Chip

The yuckiest vegetable: broccoli.

Favourite pizza toppings: ham and sausage

You can't leave home without nail polish

What is your best physical feature?

my green eyes

What is your guilty pleasure?

Eavesdropping on my father's phone conversations when he's speaking to famous clients.

What is your favourite movie?

Breakfast at Tiffany's

What is your pet peeve? People who wear jogging bottoms in public!

What doesn't come easily to you?

Wearing the same outfit twice.

If you found £10 on the street, what would you do with the money?

Buy a new lip gloss.

How would you react if someone copied your work?

I would ask my friends what I should do.

What most often gets you in trouble?

Talking too much in class.

Favourite season: Autumn, because of the fashion!

AMY

Do you speak any languages besides English? nope

Where do you want to live when you grow up? Milan

If you were stranded on a desert island, which three things would you want

to have with you? Why?

1. my super-deluxe portable make-up bag
(instant camouflage!)

2. my sketchbook (I'm sure there's lots of
fashion inspiration on desert islands.)

3. my mum's killer pointy Jimmy Choo boots
that almost fit me (to ward off predators)

What did you do over the summer?

I went with my mum to Mozambique.

Inside Amy's Bag:

You can definitely tell a lot about a girl by looking inside...

LUNCH MONEY
Just in case the canteen is serving anything edible

???

HAIR PRODUCTS
To keep my curls in check

LIP GLOSS
To keep my lips soft (just in case Ryan Hudson wants to kiss me)

FASHION MAGAZINES
So I'm in the know on the latest trends

SKETCHBOOK
You never know when fashion inspiration will strike!

PENCILS
'Cause I have to do schoolwork sometimes

CHOCOLATES
For sweet-tooth emergencies

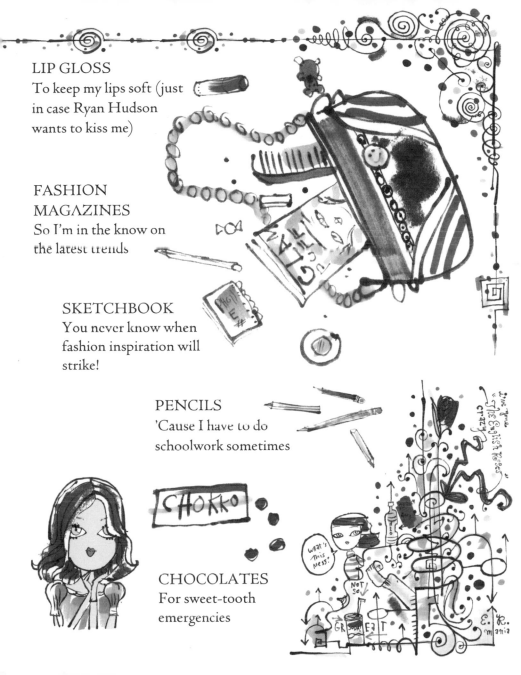

{ Vital Statistics }

Full name: Charlotte Ginsberg

Nickname: Charlie

Birthday: 4 September

Astrological sign: Virgo

Birthplace: London

Eye colour: Brown   **Hair colour:** Black

Height: 152.5 cm

Family: Parents, Nigel and Olivia; older sister, Emma; younger brother, Patrick

Pet(s): A pony named Posie

CHARLOTTE

Who is your BFF? The English Roses and my diary.

Name one thing that you can do better than any of your friends.

Ride a horse.

What is the best gift you ever received? A designer handbag.

When you grow up, what do you want to be?

A socialite, like my mum.

You can't wait till the day you can go
to a debutante ball.

Worst habit:

Doing my homework at the last minute.

What is one secret about you that only your closest friends know?

That I'm very self-conscious
about dancing.

What is the most embarrassing thing that ever happened to you?

Once I was daydreaming when a new teacher asked our names in class. When it was my turn to answer, I said my crush's name by mistake!

Heroes: Hilary Duff

Person/People you'd like to meet: Daniel Radcliffe

Celebrity crush: Daniel Radcliffe

Real-life crush: William Worthington

IM name: Charlotte

What nail polish shade are you wearing today? I have a French manicure.

# CHARLOTTE

Are your ears pierced? *no*

If you had to choose, which do you think best describes your personal style?

    a. Sporty   b. Funky   c. Casual   (d. Classic)   e. Dressy

Which best describes your personality?

    (a. Girly girl)   b. Tomboy   c. Studious   d. Fashionable   e. Goofy

Favourite lip gloss flavour: *Seashell, by Chanel*

Fashion icon: *my mother*

Favourite colour: *pink*

If your shoes did the talking, what would they say about you?

That I am very stylish and posh.

How do you want to celebrate your next birthday?

High tea at Claridge's with the English Roses, and then shopping at Harrods.

What is your favourite thing in your room? My walk-in wardrobe

When you can't fall asleep, what do you

think about? Riding Posie in the

Olympics.

Favourite way to spend a rainy afternoon·

shopping

Car you would like to drive someday:

a pink Aston Martin

Favourite book: The Famous

Five series

Three things you can't live without: hairdryer, lip gloss,

pink Prada pen case

Which is your favourite subject at school, and which do you like least?

History is brill, but I hate biology.

CHARLOTTE

Whom do you sit next to at school?

Binah and Grace.
PE is AWFUL – I
always break my nails!

What sports do you play?

None, but I love
riding horses.

Who is your favourite teacher?

Miss Fluffernutter

What do you like to do after school?

shop

What is your favourite after-school snack?

tea with scones and clotted cream

Favourite food: sushi

The yummiest ice cream flavour: pistachio

The yuckiest vegetable: cabbage

Favourite pizza toppings: artichokes

You can't leave home without splashing on some Jean
Paul Gaultier perfume.

What is your best physical feature? my hair

What is your guilty pleasure?

Eating Fruit Pastilles in bed at night.

CHARLOTTE

What is your favourite movie? That's easy – The Princess Diaries.

What is your pet peeve? sloppiness

What doesn't come easily to you? ignoring gossip

If you found £10 on the street, what would you do with the money? Not much! Oh well, buy some sweets, I guess.

How would you react if someone copied your work? I'd be proud that they thought I was so smart!

What most often gets you in trouble? Spending my pocket money too quickly.

Favourite season: Autumn

Do you speak any languages besides English? Yes, French.

Where do you want to live when you grow up? Paris

If you were stranded on a desert island, which three things would

you want to have with you? Why?

A hairbrush, a mirror
and some lip gloss, so
that I look good when
I'm rescued!

What did you do over the summer?

My family went to our villa
in the south of France,
where we go every year.

Charlotte's Etiquette
For Beginners

The English Roses always tease me about the fact that my parents sent me to charm school when I was little, but I think that good etiquette should be an important part of anyone's lifestyle. Follow the simple rules below, and you'll be the toast of the town!

Cheers!

POSTURE MAKES PERFECT

I hate to sound like your mum, but have you ever caught your reflection in the mirror when slouching? It looks simply dreadful! Try this: stand with your shoulders back, head held high, chest out and tummy tucked in. Don't you feel better already? Correct posture improves breathing and mental capabilities; it also makes you look taller and feel confident.

BORROWING BASICS

The English Roses love to borrow one another's clothes – it's like having five times the wardrobe! However, whenever you borrow anything from a friend – be it a dress or a DVD – it's important to return it in the same condition as it was when you received it. In the case of the English Roses, we always wash, iron and neatly fold the clothing we borrow from one another.

MEALTIME MATTERS

Good table manners are essential in making a positive impression. Always chew with your mouth closed, and swallow your food before speaking. Place a napkin on your lap to catch any food spills, and be sure to ask fellow diners to pass dishes not within your reach. And please don't pick food from your teeth at the table – wait until after the meal to pick in private. *Bon appétit!*

SMILE – IT'S CONTAGIOUS!

It's amazing what a simple smile can do to brighten up someone else's day – and your own! The act of smiling makes your brain produce endorphins, substances that give you a natural sense of peace and well-being. Just another reason to flash your pearly whites more often.

COLE

{ Vital Statistics }

Full name: Nicole Sophie Rissman

Nickname: Nikki

Birthday: 14 July

Astrological sign: Cancer

Birthplace: Paris, France

Eye colour: Blue   Hair colour: Dirty blonde

Height: 145 cm

Family: Mum and Daddy

Pet(s): The cutest, smartest Jack Russell terrier in the whole world, Aston

 # NICOLE

Who is your BFF? Charlotte, Grace, Amy and Binah.

Name one thing that you can do better than any of your friends.

Actually, there are two: writing and dancing.

What is the best gift you ever received? My autographed Harry Potter boxed set.

When you grow up, what do you want to be?

A writer.

You can't wait till the day you publish my first book.

Worst habit: I bite my nails and chew my pencils.

What is one secret about you that only your

closest friends know? I'm always afraid that my daddy will make us move again.

What is the most embarrassing thing that ever happened to you? I was swimming with a friend and this way-cute guy swam over to us. We started chatting and splashing around. At one point, I dived underwater, but when I came back up he gave me a funny look and quickly swam away. I couldn't figure out what was wrong. Later I realized I had had a huge gob of snot hanging out of my nose. I wanted to die.

NICOLE

Heroes: My nana, Hazel Rissman

Person/People you'd like to meet:
J.K. Rowling

Celebrity crush: Joel Madden

Real-life crush: Brent Robertson, the cutest boy in school

IM name: TruBluNik14

What nail polish shade are you wearing today?
Glum Plum

Are your ears pierced? Of course — twice.

If you had to choose, which do you think best describes your personal style?

a. Sporty   (b. Funky)   c. Casual   d. Classic   e. Dressy

Which best describes your personality?

in-between

a. Girly girl b. Tomboy c. Studious d. Fashionable e. Goofy

Favourite lip gloss flavour: Cola

Fashion icon: Avril Lavigne

Favourite colour: deeeeep navy blue

If your shoes did the talking, what would they say about you?

That I should stop writing on them (I doodle on my trainers).

How do you want to celebrate your next birthday?

A dance party that I DJ myself, with my bestest friends (and Joel Madden, LOL!).

 # NICOLE

What is your favourite thing in your room? My magic eight ball that predicts the future.

When you can't fall asleep, what do you think about? I imagine life when I'm older, living on my own as a famous writer in New York.

Favourite way to spend a rainy afternoon: reading in my room

Car you would like to drive someday: a navy blue Vespa scooter with matching helmet

Favourite book: Harriet the Spy

Three things you can't live without: CDs, the purple scarf I knitted myself, my computer

Which is your favourite subject at school, and which do you like least?

Favourite: writing. Least: a tie between maths and PE.

Whom do you sit next to at school?

Amy

PE is a total waste of

my time.

What sports do you play? As if!

None.

Who is your favourite teacher?

Miss Fluffernutter

What do you like to do after school?

read, go online, listen

to music, hang out

with my friends

What's your favourite after-school

snack? tortilla chips and spicy salsa

71

 # NICOLE

Favourite food: Indian

The yummiest ice cream flavour: dairy =
double yuck. But I do like
dairy free ice cream.

The yuckiest vegetable:
cauliflower = triple yuck!

Favourite pizza toppings: I will only
eat pizza that has green
peppers, mushrooms and
no cheese.

You can't leave home without lip gloss
and my iPod.

What is your best physical feature?
I don't have one.

What is your guilty pleasure? Watching Doctor Who episodes and Shirley Temple movies.

What is your favourite movie? The Horse Whisperer.

What is your pet peeve? Smart girls who act dumb to impress boys

What doesn't come easily to you? laughing

If you found £10 on the street, what would you do with the money? Buy a CD.

How would you react if someone copied your work? I'd poke their eyes out with a pencil!

What most often gets you in trouble? My moodiness.

Favourite season: Winter

Do you speak any languages besides English? Je parle français. (I speak French.)

NICOLE

Where do you want to live when you grow up? New York

If you were stranded on a desert island, which three things would you want

to have with you? Why? My iPod, because I can't

live without music; a

notebook, so I could

write about being

stranded on an island;

the lucky pen my nana

gave me, because I

can't write without it.

What did you do over the summer?

I went to New York

for a month with my

daddy and mum.

Nicole's Study Tips

y friends often refer to me as the brains in the group, but the truth is that I'm no more brainy than they are – I've just developed good study habits. Try these out. They're sure to work for you too.

DON'T PROCRASTINATE

Do your homework as soon as you get home – after a yummy snack, of course. That way you'll have the rest of the evening to chat on the phone, watch the telly or do any old thing you want to do.

USE FLASH CARDS

I know it sounds babyish, but it really helps to write key points on flash cards for easy reference or last-minute cramming.

DO PRACTICE TESTS

Ask your teacher or older brothers and sisters for tests from previous years. This will give you an idea of what to expect and, if you're in luck, some of the questions may even be repeated.

PLAY SOME MUSIC

(Softly, though, and in the background.) Unlike the TV, which is a huge distraction, I always find that music helps me focus when I'm doing homework. At first my parents thought I was just slacking — as if!

TAKE BREAKS

You won't get anything done if you're tired, so tear yourself away from the computer before your eyes turn googly, and stop writing before your hand cramps up.

Hola, Señorita!

Greetings from Alájar! It's a little strange for me to be back in Spain after such a long time. I keep using English words in school! I'm really happy to be with my *mamá* and *papá* again, though, and to be eating homemade paella and frittatas instead of steak and kidney pie. I don't miss English food, but I do miss the English Roses, especially you — I hope you'll come and visit me soon. In the meanwhile, tell me what everyone has been up to. Is Grace on the football team again this year? And is Nicole still planning to write a song for the talent competition? What about Amy and Charlotte? I can't wait to hear all the news.

Adiós and XO,

Dominic

To:

Binah Rossi

12 Tulip Square

London WS7 52J

United Kingdom

Stick or draw your image here

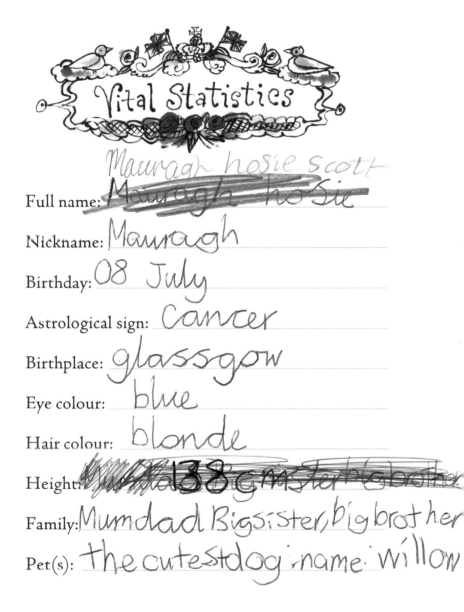

Vital Statistics

Full name: ~~Mauragh hosie scott~~ ~~Mauragh hosie~~

Nickname: Mauragh

Birthday: 08 July

Astrological sign: Cancer

Birthplace: glassgow

Eye colour: blue

Hair colour: blonde

Height: ~~138cm~~

Family: Mum dad Big sister, big brother

Pet(s): the cutest dog name willow

Who is your BFF? ~~Jessica Lucia Catriona~~ *Kelly*

Name one thing that you can do better than any of your friends.

~~my middle name~~ ~~being bonkers~~
they say drawing and careing

What is the best gift you ever received?

~~a camrer / my dog from my mum~~

When you grow up, what do you want to be? Save animals. ...

You can't wait till the day you ~~go into high school~~

Worst habit: ~~picking my neils.~~

What is one secret about you that only your closest friends know?

my middle name.

What is the most embarrassing thing that ever happened to you?

about to kiss some one when i was ~~still~~ smaller.

Heroes: ~~My mum/dad~~

Person/People you'd like to meet:

~~amy mkdonervyd~~

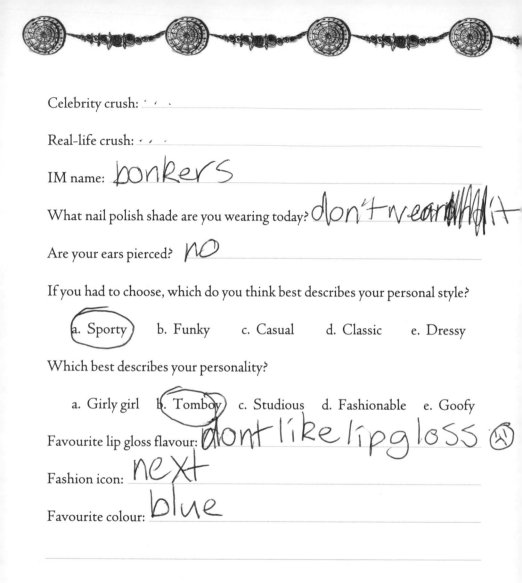

Celebrity crush: ⸌ ⸌ ⸌

Real-life crush: ⸌ ⸌ ⸌

IM name: bonkers

What nail polish shade are you wearing today? don't wear ~~it~~ it

Are your ears pierced? no

If you had to choose, which do you think best describes your personal style?

(a. Sporty)   b. Funky   c. Casual   d. Classic   e. Dressy

Which best describes your personality?

a. Girly girl   (b. Tomboy)   c. Studious   d. Fashionable   e. Goofy

Favourite lip gloss flavour: dont like lipgloss ⊗

Fashion icon: next

Favourite colour: blue

If your shoes did the talking, what would they say about you? She alawys make me mudiy.

How do you want to celebrate your next birthday? go rock climing with my friends

What is your favourite thing in your room? are music player.

When you can't fall asleep, what do you think about? What I am ~~going~~ happen tomoro.

Favourite way to spend a rainy afternoon: play with
my friends.

Car you would like to drive someday: a grey

Favourite book: the English Roses.

Three things you can't live without: my family
my friends and my dog.

Which is your favourite subject at school, and which do you like least?

I like the best/written the rost/show and tell it s soo boringg.

Whom do you sit next to at school? Jordan.

PE is fun but the teaher srickf.

What sports do you play? all of then.

Who is your favourite teacher? mr monron/mrs Robets ings.

What do you like to do after school? walk my dog . . .

What's your favourite after-school snack? cristps

Favourite food: beans on toast

The yummiest ice cream flavour: vintha

The yuckiest vegetable: cabbey.

Favourite pizza toppings: don't like pizza.

You can't leave home without

What is your best physical feature? Don't do any.

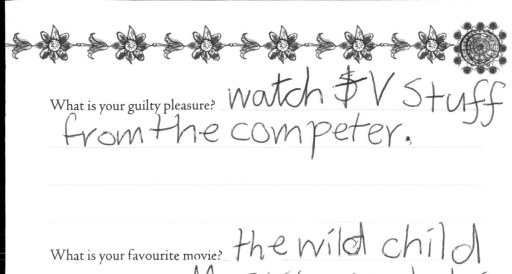

What is your guilty pleasure? watch $V stuff from the competer.

What is your favourite movie? the wild child

What is your pet peeve? My sister watching big brother / my sister.

What doesn't come easily to you? Certain types of maths.

If you found £10 on the street, what would you do with the money?

Save up for an ipod /
or give it to charerte.

How would you react if someone copied your work?

I would tell on them.

What most often gets you in trouble? Fighting with
my sister.

Favourite season: Autumn

Do you speak any languages besides English? a wee bit offerch

Where do you want to live when you grow up? ···

If you were stranded on a desert island, which three things would you want

to have with you? Why? my mum / my dad
✓ and a boat

What did you do over the summer? we stad at
mum's / and then dad's.

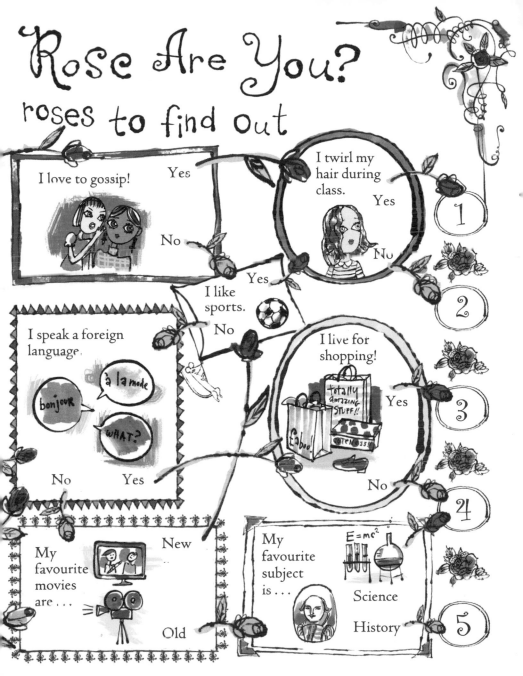

YOU ARE SOOO... ?

1

AMY:
Funky and forever unique, your flair for fashion has won you admirers near and far. You're never afraid to speak your mind, which gets you in trouble sometimes; but your friends appreciate your pure heart and fierce loyalty.

2

CHARLOTTE:
Prim and proper through and through, your perfect day involves sipping tea and shopping with your mum. Though others may think you're all about appearance, on the inside you're a very sensitive, caring person.

3 BINAH:

Soft-spoken and as gentle as a bird, you'd rather spend an evening reading about Queen Elizabeth than poring over fashion magazines. Your innate wisdom makes you the go-to girl for friends with problems.

4 NICOLE:

Others may say you're dark and moody, but on the inside you're all mushy. You brood around town with your iPod, scribbling in notebooks and daydreaming about intellectual pursuits; but you're never too busy to gossip with your friends.

5 GRACE:

You'd rather spend a day on the football field than shop and, though you hate to admit it, boys who can score a goal make your day. You may have a tough exterior, but on the inside you have a soft spot for romantic movies. Your friends always appreciate how much you try to protect them.

MADONNA RITCHIE was born in Bay City, Michigan, and now lives in London and Los Angeles with her husband, movie director Guy Ritchie, and her children, Lola, Rocco and David. She has recorded 17 albums and appeared in 18 movies. This is the first in her series of chapter books. She has also written six picture books for children, starting with the international bestseller *The English Roses*, which was released in 40 languages and more than 100 countries.

ALSO BY MADONNA:

The English Roses
Mr Peabody's Apples
Yakov and the Seven Thieves
The Adventures of Abdi
Lotsa de Casha
The English Roses: Too Good To Be True

JEFFREY FULVIMARI was born in Akron, Ohio. He started colouring when he was two, and has never stopped. Soon after graduating from The Cooper Union in New York City, he began drawing for magazines and television commercials around the globe. He currently lives in a log cabin in upstate New York, and is happiest when surrounded by stacks of paper and magic markers.

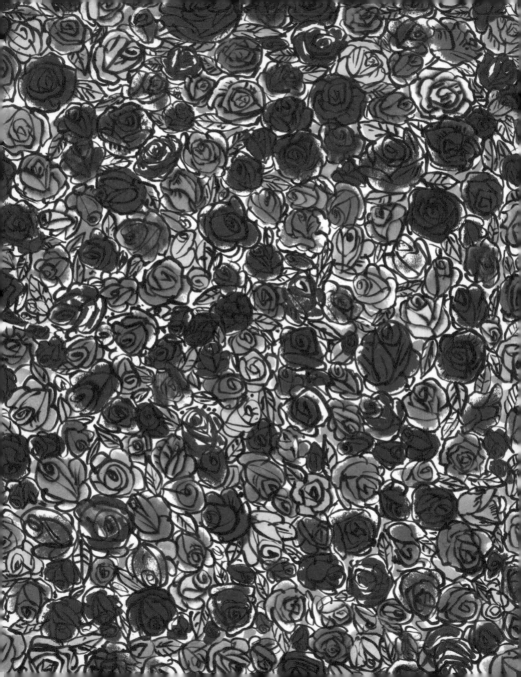

HELLO

We're the English Roses – Binah, Grace, Amy, Charlotte and Nicole. We're best friends who do everything together.

On the last day of school last year, our awesome year-seven teacher, Miss Fluffernutter, suggested we make a book listing all of our favourite things, people and memories. She told us that she and her friends made a similar book when they were our age, and she loves looking at it now. Well, we think anything Miss Fluffernutter does is the coolest, so all summer we passed this book around to one another and recorded everything – our biggest crushes, our favourite ice cream flavours, and especially our hopes and dreams for the future. We also included some special sections, like study tips, a British glossary for Grace, and a peek inside fashionista Amy's bag — even a postcard from foreign-exchange cutie Dominic de la Guardia!

We hope you have as much fun reading our book as we've had making it!

Cheers,

Binah Grace Amy
Charlotte Nicole

The Stars: the English Roses

Binah
the serious one

Grace
the sporty one

Amy
the fashionista

Charlotte
the posh one

Nicole
the brainiac

Supporting Cast

Miss Fluffernutter
the coolest teacher ever

Fairy Godmother
the sassy one

Mr Rossi
Binah's papa

**Dominic
de la Guardia**
the heartthrob

Bunny Love & Candy Darling
the dancing duo

Timmy Ferguson
the big brother

Terry Ferguson
the naughty brother

**Taffy & Tricky
Ferguson**
the twins

Mr Ferguson
the fiddle-playing
father

The Queen
everyone's favourite monarch